Copyright © 2001 by Nord-Süd Verlag AG, Gossau Zürich, Switzerland.
First published in Switzerland under the title *Ochs und Esel*.
English translation copyright © 2001 by North-South Books Inc.
All rights reserved. No part of this book may be reproduced or
utilized in any form or by any means, electronic or mechanical, including
photocopying, recording, or any information storage and retrieval
system, without permission in writing from the publisher.

First published in the United States, Great Britain, Canada,
Australia, and New Zealand in 2001 by North-South Books,
an imprint of Nord-Süd Verlag AG, Gossau Zürich, Switzerland.
Distributed in the United States by North-South Books Inc., New York.

Library of Congress Cataloging-in-Publication Data is available.
A CIP catalogue record for this book is available from The British Library.
ISBN 0-7358-1515-1 (trade binding)
1 3 5 7 9 TB 10 8 6 4 2
ISBN 0-7358-1516-X (library binding)
1 3 5 7 9 LB 10 8 6 4 2
Printed in Belgium

For more information about our books, and the authors and artists
who create them, visit our web site: www.northsouth.com

# The Ox and the Donkey

A CHRISTMAS STORY BY GÜNTER SPANG

ILLUSTRATED BY LOEK KOOPMANS

TRANSLATED BY MARIANNE MARTENS

## NORTH-SOUTH BOOKS

NEW YORK · LONDON

In the stable at the inn in Bethlehem lived an ox and a donkey. The stable was cold and drafty and sometimes wet, for the roof leaked. The ox was rude and unfriendly. Whenever the donkey wanted to snuggle up to him for warmth, the ox gave him a shove with his horns. And at mealtimes, the ox was so greedy, that there was hardly any hay left for the donkey to eat.

The ox grew fatter and fatter, but the donkey became skinnier and skinnier. Whenever the innkeeper went to the market, the donkey had to pull the heavy cart because the ox was so wild that no one could control him. It was a very hard life for the donkey, and he was sad most of the time.

Then one winter night a beautiful star rose over the broken roof, its glow lighting up the entire stable. The donkey felt as if he were under a spell. For the first time in his life his sadness left him.

Later that night a carpenter named Joseph and his wife, Mary, came into the stable. This made the donkey feel even happier and he greeted them with a loud: *"Hee-haw, hee-haw."*

Mary smiled at the donkey, and Joseph scratched him behind his ears. The donkey was overjoyed.

On this holy night, Mary gave birth to the baby Jesus.
The baby's crying made the donkey's hair stand on end.

Perhaps he is cold, thought the donkey, and he leaned
over the crib and blew gently on the baby with his warm
breath, until the baby calmed down and went to sleep.

Early the next morning, shepherds hurried in from the fields. One carried a giant bundle of hay on his back. Joseph gave some of the hay to the ox and the donkey.

It was incredible! The greedy ox let the donkey eat the largest share of the hay! And then, he actually snuggled up to the donkey and nuzzled against his shaggy coat!

That afternoon, Joseph repaired the leaky roof.
Now it was warm and snug in the stable.

The donkey and the ox took turns keeping the baby warm
with their breath.

Three Kings came to visit the Child.
The ox and the donkey hid in the furthest
corner of the stable. The smell of incense
prickled their noses and made them sneeze.
They didn't come out again until after
the Kings had left.

The three Kings had brought the baby Jesus precious gifts so, at night, the ox kept guard. He rolled his eyes and made a fearsome face to scare away any thieves who dared to approach the stable.

And the donkey waved his tail furiously to keep insects away from the baby Jesus.

Then one night Joseph and Mary packed up their belongings.
They were setting out for Egypt. The innkeeper gave Mary
bread and salt and said to Joseph: "I will lend you my
donkey. He will carry Mary and the baby Jesus to
Egypt. Once you arrive, just give him three slaps
on his rear, and he will head back home."

The donkey was happy to help. *"Hee-haw, hee-haw!"* he brayed. But the ox was very sad to see his friend go.

Carefully the donkey carried Mary and the baby Jesus all the way to Egypt. No path was too rocky, no hill too steep for him.

At home the ox waited sadly for the donkey's return. He worried that he might never see his friend again.

But then at last, the ox heard, coming from out in the fields, a loud, happy *"Hee-haw, hee-haw!"*

What joy! The innkeeper, his wife, and their son rushed to the stable to celebrate the donkey's return. And the ox and the donkey celebrated too, sharing their hay and their warmth, best friends now—and forever after.